	DATE DUE		

Raymond's Perfect Present

by Therese On Louie
illustrated by Suling Wang

Lee & Low Books · New York

Text copyright © 2002 by Therese On Louie
Illustrations copyright © 2002 by Suling Wang

Lee & Low Books Inc., 95 Madison Avenue, New York, NY 10016
www.leeandlow.com

Printed in China

Book Design by Tania Garcia
Book Production by The Kids at Our House

The text is set in Sabon
The illustrations are rendered in pencil, scanned into a computer, and
then further designed with Adobe Photoshop and a Wacom Pad.

10 9 8 7 6 5 4 3 2 1
First Edition

Library of Congress Cataloging-in-Publication Data
Louie, Therese On.
Raymond's perfect present / by Therese On Louie ; illustrated by Suling
Wang.— 1st ed.
    p. cm.
Summary: When Raymond's mother becomes sick, he remembers that
she misses the living things in the country and, with the help of their
neighbor, he tries to prepare the perfect present for her.
ISBN 1-58430-055-8
[1. Gifts—Fiction. 2. Sick—Fiction. 3. Neighbors—Fiction. 4. Flowers—
Fiction. 5. Birds—Fiction. 6. Chinese Americans—Fiction.] I. Wang,
Suling., ill. II. Title.
PZ7.L938 Ray 2002   [E]—dc21   2002016128

For my mother and Don, with love
                                    —T.O.L.

To my dad and mom, Bing and Angela,
and my brother, Howie. I am so lucky
to have grown up with all their love and
support. And to my husband, Mike, for
being my best friend and being there
with me through all the long hours
                                    —S.W.

Ever since his mother had come home from the hospital, Raymond wasn't supposed to go outside.

"It's best if you stay indoors until your mother gets better," said Mrs. Silver, who lived next door and helped Raymond and his mother. "She'll worry if you're not here."

So every day Raymond came home after school.

Inside the small apartment, it was dim and quiet. Often his mother would be asleep in her room. Raymond would grab some cookies and juice, then sit in front of his bedroom window and watch the world outside.

Many people passed by. Some walked briskly, phones held to their ears.

Men delivered boxes and furniture. Mothers pushed babies in strollers.

One day Raymond saw a man with flowers hurrying down the street. A woman appeared and the man presented her with his gift. She accepted the flowers with a smile.

Maybe I could buy Mom some flowers, thought Raymond.

Raymond's mother had once lived on a farm. She often told him about the sweet-smelling flowers that grew there, and about the birds that had tapped on her bedroom window looking for food. "I love the city, but I miss seeing all the living, growing things," she always said.

After school the next day Raymond stopped at a flower shop. The colors were dazzling! But when he held out his money, the shopkeeper shook his head.

"At that price, I'd be giving away my flowers," the shopkeeper said. "Come back with more money and I'll give you a good deal."

When Raymond got home, Mrs. Silver was warming soup for his mother. He tried not to look upset, but Mrs. Silver noticed anyway. "Raymond, what's wrong?" she asked.

So Raymond told her his plan—and his problem. Suddenly he thought of a solution.

"Seeds!" Raymond exclaimed. "The kids in Mr. Oliva's science class grew flowers. I can do that!"

"That's a nice idea," Mrs. Silver said. "Seeds don't cost much, and Mr. Silver can bring you some pots and soil."

That night Raymond was too excited to sleep. Growing flowers from seeds, what a wonderful idea!

The next day, Raymond stopped at the hardware store. A rack of seed packets displayed pictures of flowers and vegetables. He bought the seeds he wanted, then hurried home.

On the kitchen table Mrs. Silver had left him five pots, a bag of soil, two cookies, and a note. The note said "Good luck!" and had directions for planting the seeds.

Raymond ate the cookies, then carefully followed Mrs. Silver's instructions. Her note said to put the pots in the sun, so he set them on the ledge outside his window.

Raymond watered his pots every day.

Soon tiny shoots emerged from the soil. They grew taller and taller. They sprouted leaves, then bigger leaves. Finally green buds appeared and grew fat.

Raymond couldn't wait for the buds to burst into color, so he could surprise his mother. He couldn't wait for her to smile, *really* smile, and laugh again.

    Before his flowers could bloom, Raymond's
mother got worse. Mr. Silver took her back to the
hospital. Mrs. Silver helped Raymond gather some
of his things so he could stay in their apartment.

    "Don't worry," Mrs. Silver said. "The doctors
will take good care of her."

    Raymond kept his clothes folded neatly on an
armchair, did his homework without being told,
and dried the dinner dishes. Mrs. Silver asked him
questions about school. Raymond answered, but
he didn't feel like talking.

    All he could think about was his mother.

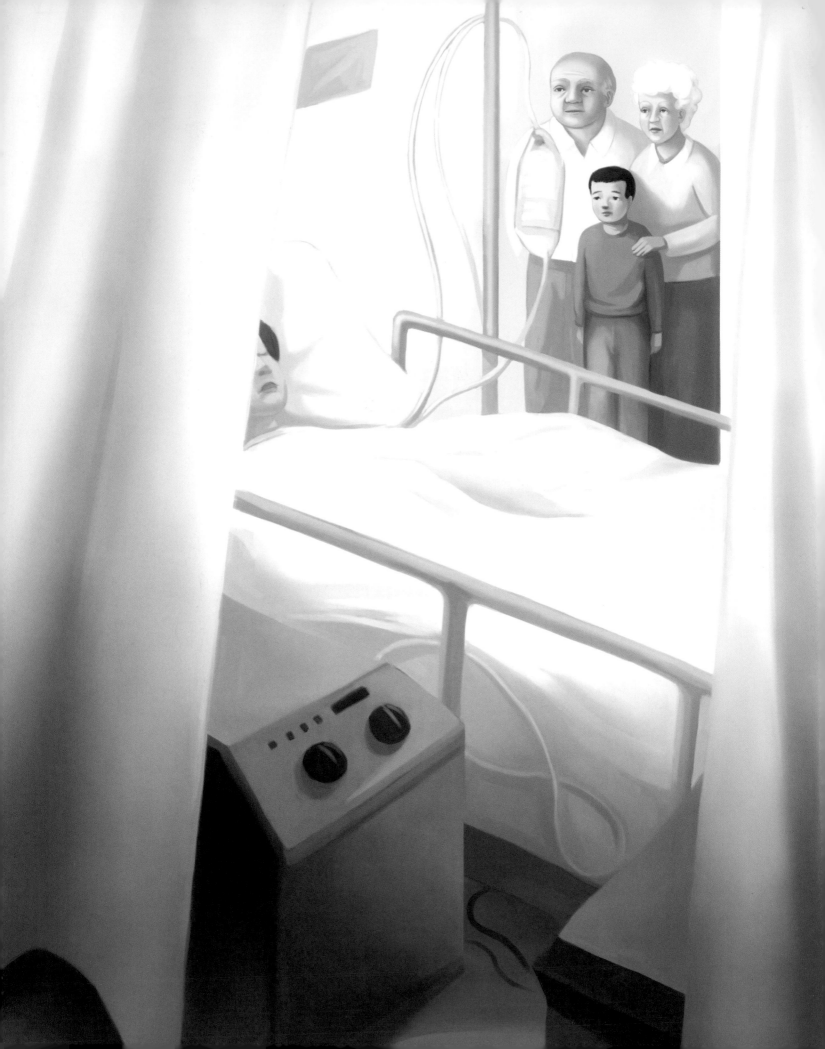

On Saturday the Silvers took Raymond to see his mother. The hospital was too bright, with funny smells and strange machines. Raymond felt small and a little scared. His mother was asleep, but woke up when they entered the room.

She looked tired and worried. "I miss you. Are you being good? Are you listening to Mr. and Mrs. Silver?"

"Yes, Mom." Raymond didn't know what else to say. Then he remembered. "Are you coming home soon? I have a surprise for you. Something I think you'll really like."

"A surprise for me? Wow." Raymond could tell his mother was trying to sound excited.

She just needs something pretty, that's all, thought Raymond as he kissed his mother good-bye. He thought of his flowers and smiled.

Even though his mother was away, Raymond still went to school. Mrs. Silver let him go home each afternoon to get clean clothes and to check on his pots. Twice a week Mr. and Mrs. Silver took Raymond to visit his mother. He always brought books to read to her.

At last the flowers began to bloom. Pink and white. Yellow and purple. Scarlet and orange. Busy insects landed and departed with a blur of wings. Butterflies

unrolled their long tongues to sample the nectar.

Raymond invited the Silvers to see the cheerful display. "It's lovely," said Mrs. Silver. "Your mother will be so pleased."

Each day more flowers opened. Raymond moved his pots to the ledge outside his mother's bedroom window. He sat on her bed and watched the insects come and go. He wished his mother were home.

A week passed. Raymond noticed that some flowers had turned brown. He ran to Mrs. Silver. "What's wrong with my flowers? Why are they sick?"

"They're not sick, Raymond. Flowers only bloom for a short time. I'm sorry that your mother isn't here to see them." Mrs. Silver put her hand on Raymond's shoulder. "But she's much better now. She'll be coming home on Sunday. I know you miss her. Won't it be nice to have her back?"

Raymond wanted his mother to come home, but Sunday was four days away. How long would his flowers last?

The next day, and the next, more flowers lost their color. Their heads drooped. Raymond felt like drooping too. He begged them to wait. "Don't die, flowers. Not now, not yet."

The flowers didn't listen. One after another, each flower's sunny face faded to brown. Dried petals fluttered to the street and scattered on the sidewalk.

Sunday finally came.

It was almost dark when the taxi arrived. Raymond and Mrs. Silver hurried downstairs to greet his mother and Mr. Silver. Raymond gave his mother a gentle hug.

She looked stronger than before. "I feel better, I really do," she said.

Raymond helped his mother get comfortable in bed. Afterward she stroked his hair. "I haven't forgotten your big surprise, Raymond," she said. "You can show it to me tomorrow."

"Well, it's not much," said Raymond. "You might not even like it." He thought of the flowers with their ugly stalks and brown heads, hidden behind the shade. If only his mother had seen them when they were beautiful!

"Of course I'll like it. I'm sure your surprise is something special," his mother said and turned off the light.

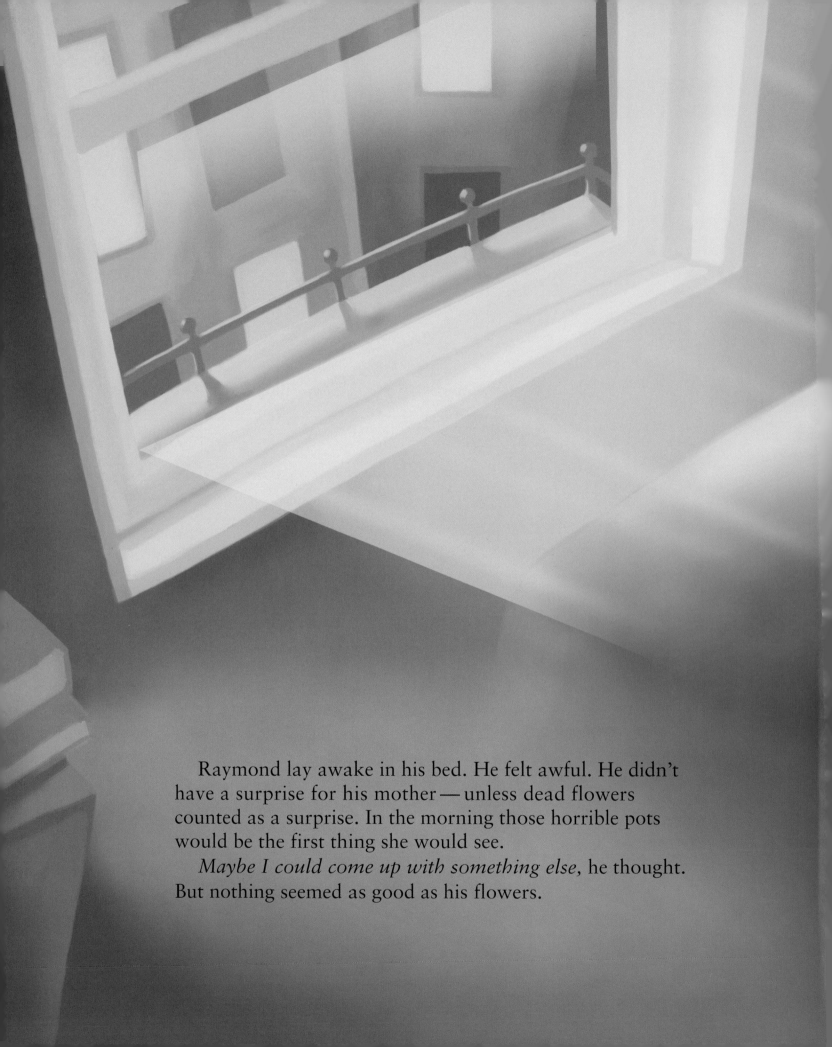

Raymond lay awake in his bed. He felt awful. He didn't have a surprise for his mother — unless dead flowers counted as a surprise. In the morning those horrible pots would be the first thing she would see.

Maybe I could come up with something else, he thought. But nothing seemed as good as his flowers.

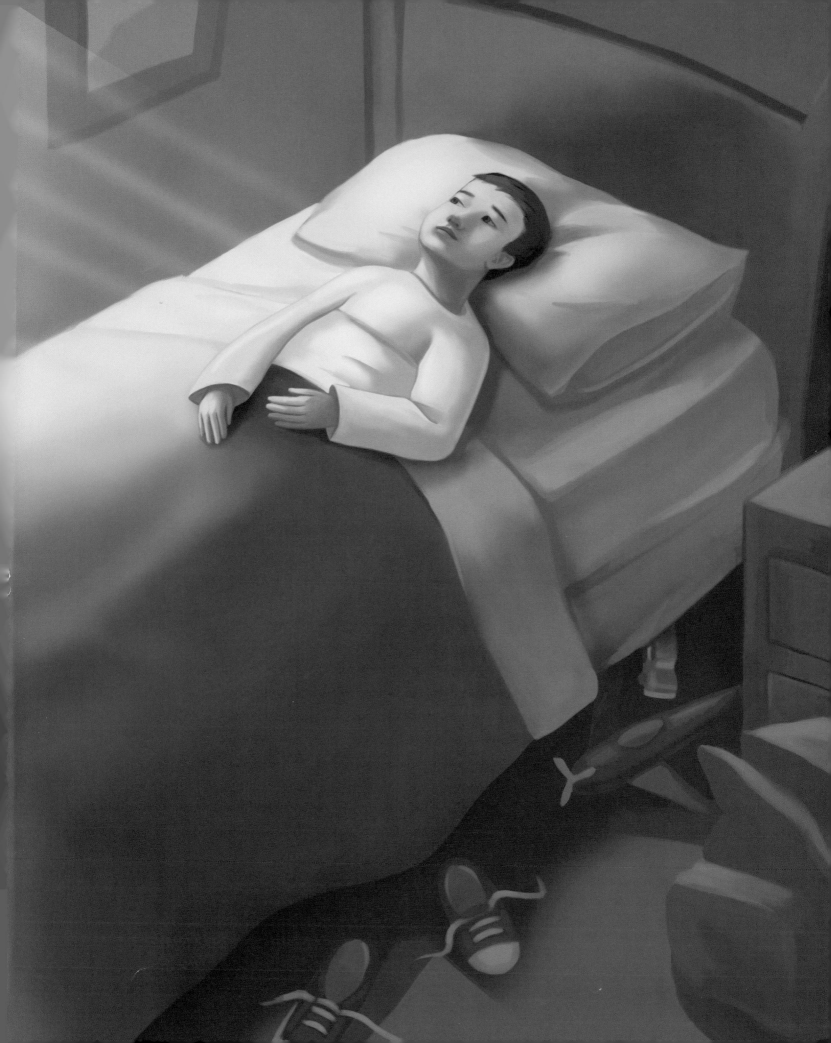

The next day the sun woke Raymond. *Morning!*
His mother must be awake.

Slowly Raymond got out of bed. He pulled
on his jeans and sweatshirt. He didn't want to go
to his mother's room. He didn't want to see her
disappointment.

His mother must have heard him. "Raymond!"
she called. "Raymond, come here." Raymond
dragged his feet down the hallway. He pushed open
the door to his mother's room.

Sunlight bounced off the white walls. Everything
in the room shone. But brightest of all was his
mother's face as she turned to him, laughing.

Raymond was confused—until he saw, behind
her, at the window . . .

Birds!

A pigeon strutted along the ledge. Small brown birds worked busily, stripping seeds from the flowers. Red-headed birds chattered and argued, then took to the air. Raymond could hear the soft sound of their beating wings through the glass.

"Oh, Raymond! This is just like when I was small and I'd wake up to birds on my windowsill! What a wonderful present!"

"It's the best surprise, isn't it, Mom?" said Raymond.

"Yes, Raymond." His mother smiled, *really* smiled. "The absolute best surprise."

That morning, and for four mornings afterward, Raymond ate breakfast sitting on his mother's bed. They watched the birds together. They talked and laughed and told stories, just like they used to.

By the following Saturday the flowers were bare of all their seeds. Not one bird came.

But that didn't matter.

On that Saturday, Raymond's mother was better —
much better — and it was a perfect day for the park.